It's Not About You, Mr. Santa Claus

A Love Letter About the True Meaning of Christmas

Soraya Diase Coffelt
Illustrated by Tea Seroya

The Love Letters Book Series

NEW YORK

It's Not About You, Mr. Santa Claus
A Love Letter About the True Meaning of Christmas

Published in New York, New York, by Morgan James Publishing. Morgan James and The Entrepreneurial Publisher are trademarks of Morgan James, LLC. www.MorganJamesPublishing.com

The Morgan James Speakers Group can bring authors to your live event. For more information or to book an event visit The Morgan James Speakers Group at www.TheMorganJamesSpeakersGroup.com.

A free eBook edition is available with the purchase of this print book.

ISBN 978-1-63047-261-0 paperback
ISBN 978-1-63047-262-7 eBook
ISBN 978-1-63047-263-4 hard cover

CLEARLY PRINT YOUR NAME ABOVE IN UPPER CASE

Instructions to claim your free eBook edition:
1. Download the BitLit app for Android or iOS
2. Write your name in **UPPER CASE** on the line
3. Use the BitLit app to submit a photo
4. Download your eBook to any device

In an effort to support local communities, raise awareness and funds, Morgan James Publishing donates a percentage of all book sales for the life of each book to Habitat for Humanity Peninsula and Greater Williamsburg.

Get involved today, visit www.MorganJamesBuilds.com.

Habitat for Humanity®
Peninsula and Greater Williamsburg
Building Partner

God told Abraham that because of his faithfulness, God would bless him and all of his descendants, who would be as numerous as the stars of the sky.
Genesis 15:5; 22:15; Hebrews 11:8-12.

Children, along with adults, are among Abraham's descendants.

Dedication

I dedicate this book to Jesus Christ, my Lord and Savior. It is because of Him that I live, move, and exist. I also dedicate this book to my late husband, Gordon and my two sons, Zachary and James. Thank you for your unconditional love and support.

Dear Santa,

2

It's Not About You, Mr. Santa Claus

Dear Mr. Santa Claus,

I t's me again—a kid. I know I've written lots of letters to you before with long lists of gifts I wanted for Christmas. Well, not this year. This letter is different.

I discovered that the real meaning of Christmas has nothing to do with you at all. It is about a very special gift. I want to tell you about this gift.

By the way, how are you and Mrs. Santa Claus doing? Have you lost any weight? Did your helpers, the elves, grow any taller? Do you still like cookies and milk? Are you still wearing that red, furry outfit? I've always wondered, what do you wear in the summer time?

I know you like to ride on your sleigh with the reindeer and give lots of presents to kids. Someone told me recently how that all got started. I was very surprised to learn it had nothing to do with you!

It's a great story that I want to share with you, so I suggest that you get a nice comfy chair and sit down and relax.

The real Christmas story began a long time ago, when a Roman emperor named Caesar Augustus ordered that a census be taken. A census is when all the people had to be counted.

At that time, a man named Joseph and his wife, Mary had to take a long journey to the city of David, known as Bethlehem, for the census.

It wasn't an easy journey as Mary was going to have a baby soon. The baby would be her first child. When they arrived in Bethlehem, they were very tired. So many people had traveled to the city for the census that there were no rooms left at the inn. The only place the innkeeper had to offer them was the stable, where all the animals were kept.

So Joseph and Mary and their donkey went to the stable to spend the night. I mention their donkey because they didn't have cars in those days. People usually rode donkeys to travel.

The stable was filled with all kinds of animals—cows, sheep, goats, donkeys, and horses. I wonder what Joseph and Mary thought about that? I think they were very grateful for a place to rest after their long trip. Of course, the donkey didn't care because he was with his own kind.

T hat night, Mary gave birth to the baby, right there in the stable. They named him Jesus, which means Savior. They laid him in a manger to sleep, because they didn't have a crib. Do you know what a manger is? It's a wooden box where food is placed for the animals to eat. I wonder if the baby was comfortable inside that manger?

Mr. Santa Claus, I learned that this baby wasn't just an ordinary baby, so the story doesn't end here. In fact, this is just the beginning. You might want to get a snack of cookies and milk now, while I tell you the rest of the story. What happens next is amazing!

Some shepherds lived in the fields near Bethlehem. I don't think you have any shepherds in the North Pole, do you? Well, let me tell you a little about shepherds. They take care of sheep and live out in the fields with them. They have a very important job because they protect the sheep from wild animals. And, they don't have to take baths or do homework. That's a good life, if you ask me!

One night, when the shepherds were out in the field, an angel suddenly appeared and a bright light surrounded them. The shepherds were surprised and scared. The angel told them not to be afraid! He proclaimed: *"I bring you good news that will bring great joy to all people."*

Do you want to know what the good news was from the angel? It was the first Gift ever given to the world! It was the baby, Jesus, who had been born in the stable! The angel called him a Savior, Christ the Lord.

He told them exactly where to find the baby, wrapped in cloth, lying in a manger. I'm sure that the shepherds would never have thought of looking for a baby in a stable!

When the angel finished speaking, many other angels appeared to the shepherds, praising God, and saying, *"Glory to God in highest heaven, and peace on earth to those with whom God is pleased."*

The shepherds were so excited to see what the angel was talking about that they ran all the way to Bethlehem to find the baby Jesus.

They didn't care that they found him in a manger surrounded by all the animals and smells in the stable. They were used to them. Besides, they smelled like them, too.

They were happy to see the baby Jesus and realized that they were part of something very special. Their hearts were filled with joy and they couldn't stop praising God and telling people what they had seen as they returned to their fields. This special baby had caused quite a stir among the shepherds. But they weren't the only ones who had heard about this special Gift.

Mr. Santa Claus, I hope you enjoyed your snack because the story gets even more exciting. Just lay back in your comfortable chair and put your feet up while I continue.

W ell, every story has a bad guy, including this one! His name was King Herod, who was the king of the region where Jesus lived. One day, some very important visitors called the Magi came to see King Herod because they were trying to find Jesus. They were considered wise men as they were smart and well respected.

The Magi had traveled a long way from their homes in the east so that they could bring gifts to Jesus and worship him. They knew that there was something very special about this kid. They brought treasure chests filled with gifts of gold, frankincense, and myrrh for Jesus.

Oh, if you didn't know, frankincense and myrrh were precious, rare, and expensive spices that were used back in those times. I think those are strange gifts for a child. But, I learned that they were worthy of a king, which is why they brought them to Jesus. They believed he was a king, but I'll get to that later.

So the Magi must have known what the angel had told the shepherds—that Jesus was the Savior of the world—because they traveled all that distance to worship him.

You may wonder how they found Jesus. That is a story in and of itself and it involves King Herod!

They followed a very bright star in the sky that led them all the way to the city of Jerusalem. When they arrived in the city, King Herod asked them to come to his palace. The Magi told King Herod that they were searching for another king who had been born and they wanted to worship him. They asked King Herod for help. Well, this made him really mad! He knew that the Magi hadn't brought him any gifts even though he was the king! And, King Herod didn't want there to be another king. He wanted to be the ONLY KING!

Immediately, King Herod wanted to kill Jesus. He came up with a plan to trick the wise men. He told them to continue searching for the child king. He asked them to let him know when they found him so that he could worship the child king, too. But, as I said, that was a lie because he really wanted to kill Jesus so that he would be the only king!

Mr. Santa Claus, fortunately, these Magi were very wise men! They didn't trust King Herod. When they left the palace to find Jesus, the bright star led them directly to the house where Jesus lived in Bethlehem. When they saw Jesus, they fell down on their knees and worshipped him and then opened their treasure chests and gave their gifts to him. God warned them in a dream not to go back to King Herod, so they left the city by a completely different route so that the king wouldn't know.

So Mr. Santa Claus, that's where the idea of giving gifts to kids really started! It all began as an act of honor and respect for the child, Jesus.

This Christmas, I want to thank you for all that you do. For every gift that you give to kids, well, it is as if you are honoring Jesus, too!

There is a lot more to this story about Jesus as you have probably guessed.

Perhaps I can write another letter soon and tell you more about it. You see, Jesus' life as he grew up and met other people, was just as unusual as his birth! And, of course, he especially loved children!

So, Mr. Santa Claus, the true meaning of Christmas is about celebrating Jesus. By the way, did you know that Christmas means "Christ" (Jesus) and "mas" (a celebration)? The story about Jesus is found in the name of that special day when we celebrate his birth! Anyway, don't worry—I won't forget you. I still love you, but I love Jesus more.

This Christmas, instead of asking you for more gifts, I've told you about the most precious gift of all. Jesus was born to be our Savior and Lord.

I decided to make Him Lord of my life. If you haven't done so already, you can too!

Love,
Me

Dear Reader,

If you want to celebrate Jesus and make Him Lord of your life, say this simple prayer:

"Dear Lord Jesus, thank you for loving me so much that You died on the cross for my sins. I ask you to be my Lord and Savior.

Amen."

About the Author

Soraya Diase Coffelt is a widow and the mother of two sons. She is a lawyer and former judge of the Territorial Court of the Virgin Islands (now renamed the Superior Court) on St. Thomas, U.S. Virgin Islands. She began as a parent volunteer in the Children's Ministry at her church, and over a period of about 15 years, became a leader and then a lay minister in the Children's Ministry. She has been on missionary trips to Honduras and the Amazon Region of Peru ministering to adults and children. God has given her many creative ideas for ministering His Word to children, and her books are among some of them.

In 2012, she established a non-profit foundation, As the Stars of the Sky Foundation, Inc., to assist with the physical and spiritual needs of children. All proceeds from the sale of her books go towards the foundation.

If you have enjoyed this book and want to learn more about Jesus'
life, I invite you to purchase a copy of another book in The Love
Letters series due out soon:

It's Not About You, Mr. Easter Bunny

It's Not About You, Mrs. Turkey

It's Not About You, Mr. Pumpkin
And more….

To order additional copies, please go to:

www.asthestarsofthesky.org

or email us: info@asthestarsofthesky.org

CPSIA information can be obtained at www.ICGtesting.com
Printed in the USA
LVOW02s1704220915

455206LV00003B/3/P